For Lesley

First U.S. edition 2013

Library of Congress Catalog Card Number 2013931464
ISBN 978-0-7636-6952-2

13 14 15 16 17 18 SFP 10 9 8 7 6 5 4 3 2 1

Printed in Shenzhen, Guangdong, China

This book was typeset in Cremona.
The illustrations were created digitally.

Nosy Crow
An imprint of
Candlewick Press
99 Dover Street
Somerville, Massachusetts 02144

www.nosycrow.com
www.candlewick.com

Princess Penelope and the Runaway Kitten

nosy crow

An imprint of Candlewick Press

Alison Murray

In Royaltown Palace one long lazy day,

Princess Penelope wanted to play.

But Daddy was reading

and Mommy was knitting,

so she thought she'd make friends

with the mischievous kitten.

Penelope giggled—the kitten looked funny

with pink yarn all tangled

around his white tummy.

But then off he ran, with a swish of his tail,
leaving behind him a pink woolly trail!
Penelope chased him, and Doggy did too.

But where was the kitten?
He'd dashed to the stairs!

Penelope followed
the trail up and down.

"Where can he be headed?"

she said with a frown.

The yarn looped toward the garden.
"I think that it's clear
my runaway kitten has
had fun out here!"

And just when the tired princess sat down with a thump,

the kitten escaped   with a skip and a jump.

Penelope followed. "Oh, please come back, Kitty!

The yarn will be ruined, and it was so pretty!"

But the kitten went scampering
past the tall trees
and on through the cabbages,
spinach, and peas.

He ran through the kitchen
and startled the cooks.

The pots banged and clanged
as they swung from their hooks.

The parlor maid squealed and dropped sweets on the floor.

Then the little white kitten dashed through a door.

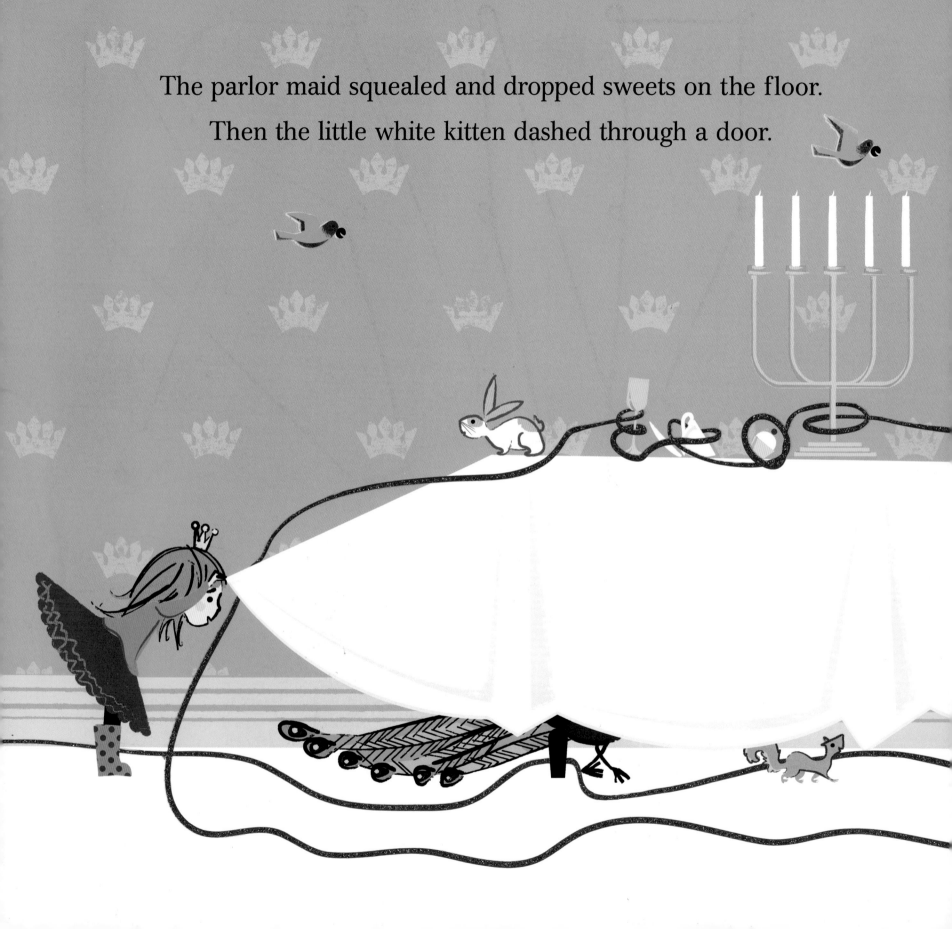

The princess said, "Now I can see why you ran off so fast!"

as the kitten curled up with his mother at last.